First published in the UK in 2023 by
Full Media Ltd
10 Oak Tree Avenue
Congleton
Cheshire
CW12 4QF

Text copyright © Jocelyn Porter, 2023
Illustrations copyright © Clare Caddy, 2023

Thanks to Helen Greathead: Editorial Adviser
Thanks also to Nick Jones for proofreading
and layout assistance

The right of Jocelyn Porter to be identified as the author and
Clare Caddy as the illustrator of this work respectively has
been asserted by them in accordance with the Copyright,
Designs and Patents Act, 1988.
All rights reserved.

This book is sold subject to the condition that it shall not,
by way of trade or otherwise, be lent, resold, hired out, or
otherwise circulated without the publisher's prior consent
in any form of binding or cover other than that in which it
is published and without a similar condition, including this
condition, being imposed upon the subsequent purchaser.

A CIP Catalogue record for this book is available from the
British Library.

ISBN: 978-1-7391244-2-7

Printed and bound in Great Britain by Clays Ltd, Elcograf S.p.A.

For Elodie Elizabeth

... may she always find magic in a book

JP

For Tilly, Reeva & Leyla

... who always make sleepovers magical

CC

For Jane
Best wishes
Jocelyn Porter

Me and My Best Friends

Sophie

Me

Charlotte

Marigold Moonglow
My Fairy Godmother

My Den

The Orchard

Puddington

Contents

An Amazing Idea

It was a warm summer afternoon and I was waiting in the café at the Buttercup Bakery for Sophie and Charlotte to arrive. We were going to have a picnic outside my den at the bottom of our garden. We have a very long garden!

Mum and Dad own the Buttercup Bakery and we live upstairs in a jumble of rooms. My bedroom is in the attic – it's a fantastic room, quite magical, as I discovered a few weeks ago. But that's old news; things are happening so rapidly these days, I can hardly keep up with them.

My den is an old wooden shed with a little grassy patch in front of it. Before you get to the grassy patch, there's an orchard. The trees in the orchard are very old, and there is something quite mysterious about them.

Unless you walk along a path that twists and turns through the trees, you can't see my den until you get there. It's a super-secret place to play.

Sophie and Charlotte arrived and I rushed to greet them. We did our usual bear hug, jumping up and down and giggling. That was until Mum chased us out of the café.

"You're disturbing my customers,"

mum scolded, handing me our picnic hamper. "Off you go and enjoy yourselves." She opened the back door and shooed us out.

Still giggling, we scurried down the orchard path and flung ourselves on the grass in front of my den. We began comparing notes about the first week of the summer term. Mr Pepper's class kept cropping up in the conversation. Mr Pepper teaches the year above us, and we're not very keen on the boys in his class.

"They're always shouting and fighting," moaned Sophie.

"I know," said Charlotte, "I keep out of their way whenever I can."

"Me too, I can't be bothered with their silliness. I just ignore them. I'm going to put them out of my mind and

3

enjoy our picnic," I said, munching a
chicken and cucumber sandwich.

That's when an idea popped into
my head. I don't know where it came
from, but the more I thought about it,
the more excited I became. I just had to
tell my friends before I exploded.

"I've had an amazing idea," I

squealed. "We could have a sleepover, right here, in my den. It would be magic; I know it would."

"Wow! That's a great idea," said Sophie, "but can we do it next week when it's my birthday? I want to do something different this year, and a sleepover in your den would definitely be different."

"I like the idea, even though it gives me the shivers," said Charlotte. "We might see an owl or a fox, or a woodland fairy, or maybe a spooky old witch. Who knows what goes on in the orchard when it's dark?" Charlotte was letting her imagination run wild, just like she always does!

We told our parents about our sleepover plan and, to our surprise, they agreed – if we promised to be good. "*No roaming round the orchard after dark,"* they said.

"Of course not," we promised, and I'm sure we really meant it. The thought of roaming round the orchard in the dark was half the fun, but it might have been too scary, especially for Charlotte with her vivid imagination!

On the evening of Sophie's eighth birthday, we rushed down to my den with a bundle of sleeping bags, pillows, pyjamas and other important things.

Mum and Dad came with us and carried our sleepover feast, which included the butterfly cupcakes I'd made specially for Sophie. You know I love baking – don't you?

I actually won a baking competition and appeared on television with a famous chef! That was amazing, but not half as amazing as when I discovered I had a fairy godmother. My life has been pretty exciting recently, and I'm certain our sleepover will be exciting too!

Anyway, Mum and Dad saw us safely inside my den and made sure I remembered to bring my phone – *"Just in case you need us!"* Then they said goodnight, and we were alone at last.

A lantern was glowing in the corner, and the walls of my dear old den had a golden glow that made it feel warm and safe.

A Noise in the Night

We laid out our party food on a little camping table, and we started nibbling sausage rolls and sandwiches, but to be honest, we were far too excited to eat very much.

Our sleeping bags looked cosy and inviting, so we changed into our pyjamas ready to snuggle down. Sophie put on her new unicorn onesie.

"It's a birthday present from my

nanna," she explained. "She still thinks I'm a little kid. She can't get used to the idea I'm all grown up now!"

"Well, you are only eight. Wait until you're eight and a half, like me, then you'll be all grown up," I said.

"Or even eight and a quarter, like me," said Charlotte with a giggle. "Don't

worry about being the youngest, Sophie. Katherine and I will look after you."

"I don't need looking after. I can look after myself, *thank you very much!*" snapped Sophie.

We had just snuggled down in our sleeping bags when there was a loud *THWACK* on the roof. My poor old shed shook and rattled like a wonky washing machine.

"Yikes! What was that?" I gasped, jumping up.

Sophie sat bolt upright, but Charlotte dived deep inside her sleeping bag.

"I'm sure it's nothing to worry about. Funny things happen in the orchard all the time," I said, crossing my fingers behind my back because that wasn't actually true.

"I'm worried, even if you aren't," sniffed Charlotte, as she popped her head out from her sleeping bag. She looked as if she was about to burst into tears.

"Never mind, it was probably just a branch falling from a tree," I said. "Come on, let's have a group hug, it will make us feel better."

I had no idea what hit the roof, but I hoped it wasn't going to spoil our sleepover, and for a few minutes, the group hug did make things feel better. That was until Charlotte's nerves got the better of her.

"It was a witch, I know it was a witch," she howled, jumping up and down. "She landed on the roof and now she's spying on us. *Look!*" Charlotte was frantically pointing at the window.

"Don't be silly, that's not a witch,"
I said. "It's just the shadow of a tree.
There are *no* witches in my orchard.
Anyway, there is nothing wrong with
witches. I'm sure most of them are very
nice."

"I'm not being silly," replied
Charlotte, stamping her foot. "You said
there were no fairies in the orchard
until you discovered you had a fairy
godmother."

"That's different," I replied.
"Marigold's not an ordinary fairy, she's
a woodland fairy and woodland fairies
are just like people, except they can do
magic."

"You said Marigold was going
to arrange a magical treat for us, but
I think she's forgotten all about it,"
moaned Sophie. "Anyway, I don't believe

you have a fairy godmother! We've never seen her. I think you made her up."

"I *do* have a fairy godmother," I protested. "I really do! And Marigold would never forget a promise, I'm sure of that."

Everything was back to normal; we were arguing about witches and fairies again. We do that all the time.

This was the first time I'd been in my den after dark, and everything had been going well until that *thing* hit the roof. It scared Charlotte and Sophie, but it didn't scare me! It made me jump, but that's not being scared – *is it*?

Chapter Three

Summer Snow

A few days earlier, Marigold had said, "*Sophie's birthday will be the perfect time for the magical treat I promised you. I'll come to your den when you have your sleepover. But don't tell the girls, let's surprise them!*"

It had been difficult keeping that secret to myself, and I was longing to blurt it out. As every minute ticked by, I was getting more impatient. I looked at the time on my phone. It was 21.30 and the sun had set and been replaced by a beautiful full moon. It was a perfect night for our sleepover.

I hope Marigold turns up soon, or we'll be asleep before she gets here, I thought to myself, then, without realising it, I mumbled out loud, "She's probably stopped to talk to a tree."

"Who's talking to a tree?" asked Sophie.

"Nobody," I said, realising I'd nearly given the game away. "I'm going outside to see what hit the roof."

"We're not allowed in the orchard after dark. We promised," Sophie reminded me.

"Oh, *snickerdoodles!*" I groaned. "I'll just open the door then. Maybe I'll see something."

I grabbed my torch and shone the light outside.

"Wow!" I cried out in delight. "The orchard's covered in snow."

"Stop messing about," snapped Sophie. "We're not falling for that. It's summer. It doesn't snow in summer."

"I'm not messing about! There really is thick snow outside," I said. "Come and see for yourselves."

The girls could hardly believe their eyes, and in a flash, we had tumbled out of the den, and were running round whooping for joy. The soft layer of snow was shining in the bright moonlight, and although I was wearing my slippers, my feet didn't feel cold or wet. Even the snowballs we started throwing at each other felt warm. It was all very odd.

17

"Gotcha," giggled Sophie as
a snowball landed on my head. We
completely forgot about staying in the
den. We were too busy enjoying our
snowball fight.

Coloured lights suddenly
appeared in the trees and started
moving towards us. We stopped
throwing snowballs instantly.

"Oh my! What's that doing here?"

I said, rubbing my eyes to make sure I wasn't dreaming.

Rolling through the snow was the land train from Puddington Pleasure Park. I recognised the big blue elephant at the front. It was Elroy! Not only that, someone was in the driver's cab and they were waving like mad.

"It's Marigold!" I shrieked. "She's here at last."

Marigold leapt down and gave me a hug.

"Sorry we hit your roof," she said. "We were flying too low when we came in to land and we finished up in the trees."

"I thought it might be you," I said with a sigh of relief.

"We took a detour over the North Pole on our way here. Elroy grabbed a snow cloud with his trunk," laughed Marigold. "He thought Sophie might like some snow on her birthday, but he took the precaution of warming it up; he didn't want you to get cold before your adventure began."

I looked at my friends. They were standing like statues, eyes wide open and gasping for air.

Chapter Four

Shock Announcement

"This is Marigold Moonglow, my fairy godmother," I said, grinning like a Cheshire cat.

"Hello, girls. I'm delighted to meet you at last. Katherine has told me so much about you," said Marigold. "Sophie's birthday seemed the perfect time to keep my promise, so I'm going to take you all on a magical adventure tonight!"

Charlotte was making funny little squeaking noises, and Sophie was shivering with excitement. "Where are we going?" she asked shyly.

"We're going to Oak Tree Hollow," Marigold explained. "It's a pretty little village in Fairyland. A magical carnival always arrives in Oak Tree Hollow when there's a full moon. I've told my fairy friends it's your birthday, and they'll be waiting to greet you when we arrive."

"Wowee! I love carnivals," shrieked Sophie. "Will there be hot dogs and candyfloss, and lots of loud music?"

"Yes, there will, and a surprise for the birthday girl," said Marigold with a wink. "But we need to get going. Don't worry when the train takes off. It can be scarily exciting if you're not used to flying, but it's completely safe."

"You mean we're going to fly in that thing?" gasped Charlotte, pointing to the land train.

"Of course," said Marigold. "It's perfect for a birthday adventure."

"I won't be scared. I'm eight today," declared Sophie.

"I won't be scared either," said Charlotte, but she had a little wobble in her voice.

"I know *you* won't be scared," said Marigold, staring at me, her eyes twinkling with a mischievous gleam. "All you have to do is squeeze your earlobe and say *snickerdoodles*, and you'll be able to cope with anything."

"I already squeeze my earlobe when I'm thinking," I said, "but why do I have to say *snickerdoodles*?"

I knew Marigold was going to tell

me something important.

"You have to say *snickerdoodles* because it's a word you like saying, and now it's the magic word you have to say when you want to cast a spell, my little witch."

"*Witch*? What do you mean? I'm not a witch," I gulped.

"I'm afraid you are, Katherine,

but I'll explain everything later," said Marigold, putting a finger to her lips and turning her attention to the adventure ahead.

"Snippety clickety," said Marigold, snapping her fingers, and in a flash, we found ourselves in the train carriage. It was decorated with a banner that said, "Happy Birthday Sophie".

I should have been happy, but I was worried. I'd seen a horrified look flash between Charlotte and Sophie when Marigold said I was a witch.

What if they believed her? What would they do? I hoped Marigold was only teasing – in fact, I was sure she was!

Chapter Five

Mischievous Moonbeams

I could see Elroy's ears flapping as we rose into the air, and his trunk was swinging from side to side.

"I fly with Elroy as often as I can. We have such fun together in the night sky," said Marigold. "Elroy loves children; he's thrilled to be part of Sophie's birthday adventure."

"Hello, everyone!" boomed Elroy. "Happy Birthday, Sophie."

"Thank you, Elroy," gasped Sophie, then she turned to me and whispered, "A big blue elephant just wished me a happy birthday."

"Of course he did," I said, as if it was nothing special. "It's all part of your birthday adventure."

Sophie grinned sheepishly. "Oh my! This is so strange; it feels like a dream."

"Well, it's not a dream, this is actually happening," I said.

"It's time to get you into something more suitable for an adventure. Can't have you wandering around in your pyjamas," said Marigold. Marigold clicked her fingers, and in a flash, we were back in our day clothes.

I couldn't resist leaning out of the window as we flew over Puddington. I could see the street lights twinkling far below us.

"Watch out for mischievous moonbeams. They will try to trick you if you don't keep an eye on them," called Marigold from the driver's cab.

A few minutes later, a beam of light slipped into our carriage. It looked more like a fine chiffon scarf than a moonbeam, but we guessed this must be one of those mischievous ones that Marigold had warned us about!

"Mmmm, I can smell scrumptious hot dogs; it's making me feel hungry," murmured Sophie as the moonbeam draped itself round her shoulders. "It tickles," she giggled, twirling round with the moonbeam swishing behind her.

"You'd better watch out," said Charlotte, "that moonbeam may try to trick you."

"You're just jealous," laughed Sophie.

"No, I'm not! *You're* the birthday girl! It's your special day; I don't want to be tickled by a moonbeam!"

As we flew over Puddington Pleasure Park, I caught sight of something leaving the ground. Minutes later, the sound of a fairground organ floated into the carriage. A carousel was hovering beside the train!

"I wish I could ride on that carousel," said Sophie. "When we go to the Pleasure Park I always ride on the carousel. I love it."

"Don't be silly, carousels can't fly. It must be some sort of hologram," snorted Charlotte. "I learnt about holograms at school last week. They're an intrusion, they're not real."

"You mean an illusion, not intrusion," said Sophie. "Anyway, I'm not going to argue with you; you can believe what you want. It's my birthday and I'm going to ride on that carousel, hologram or not!"

"I'm not sure that's possible," I said. "Perhaps it will follow us to Oak Tree Hollow. You can ride on it there."

"I hope you are right," sighed Sophie.

Chapter Six

The Unexpected Passenger

Suddenly the mischievous moonbeam
started wrapping itself round Sophie.
It grew longer and longer, until it had
covered her from head to toe! Sophie
looked like a large, white cocoon.

    With Sophie a helpless prisoner,
the moonbeam started to glide towards
the window. I panicked. I thought it was
going to float right out of the carriage,
taking Sophie with it. I squeezed my

earlobe and shouted "*Snickerdoodles! Moonbeam, stop!*"

The moonbeam stopped instantly, untangled itself from Sophie and dropped her on the floor. Then it did a cheeky little shimmy and shot out of the window.

"Wow, thank goodness for that," I gasped. But my mind was in turmoil. Had the moonbeam dropped Sophie because of my command? If that spell worked, did it mean I was a witch? *Of course not*, I told myself. *The moonbeam just happened to drop Sophie at that moment. It had nothing to do with me.*

But before I had time to say anything, Sophie jumped up. Quick as a flash, she followed the moonbeam out of the window, jumped on the carousel and climbed on a horse. The moonbeam

reappeared and draped itself round her
shoulders again.

Sophie waved to us. "Bye-bye!"
she giggled, and the carousel began to
turn and drift away.

"Oh dear, I wasn't expecting that," I gasped, flopping down on a seat. "What am I going to tell Sophie's mum? I can't just say, '*We lost Sophie*', can I, Charlotte?"

Charlotte snorted. "If warts start growing on your nose, don't expect me to be your friend anymore." She had a scowl on her face. "I don't like witches, and something smells very witchy round here. What have you done with Sophie, you horrible witch?"

I was horrified. I'm not a witch and I'm not horrible.

"I don't know what's happening," I protested.

"Don't worry, Sophie's under a spell," Marigold called from the driver's cab. "The mischievous moonbeam has made her feel giddy and full of fun.

She'll be back soon, unless the weather changes. I thought I saw some storm clouds in the distance."

I was about to ask Marigold what she meant when Charlotte mumbled *"Oo-er!"* in a very strange voice. She was pointing at something behind me.

I turned round to see a cowboy grinning at me.

"Oh no!" I snorted in disgust. "It's Charlie Broccoli from Mr Pepper's class. What's he doing on our train, Marigold?"

"I thought you might need

some help getting Sophie back, just in case the storm arrives," said Marigold. "Charlie's the perfect person for that."

"We don't need help from any boy," I snapped. "We don't talk to the boys in Mr Pepper's class. They're mean to us and they're always fighting."

"I'm not like the other boys," said Charlie. "I'm learning to be an actor. I've already been in one film. I'm sure I can help you – if you want me to."

I wasn't convinced. I was not sure how being an actor could help us find Sophie, but, as Marigold had brought Charlie here by magic, I thought I should at least give him a chance.

Chapter Seven

Dylan to the Rescue

"Have you seen my film?" asked Charlie.

"Don't think so," I said. "Anyway, I wouldn't remember seeing you in anything."

"Neither would I," piped up Charlotte.

Charlie didn't seem to notice we were being rude. He took a deep breath and began talking rapidly.

"I was a cowboy in a film called

The Attack of the Fire-Breathing Goblins.
I helped save the world. One of the
goblins set my hair on fire. He said it
was an accident, but I know he did it
deliberately."

"I've definitely not seen it," I said.

"Neither have I," said Charlotte.
"I'd remember a film about fire-
breathing goblins. I don't like goblins –
not that I've ever met one."

"I have," said Charlie, "and I don't
like them. They have a habit of farting
when you don't expect it, and they smell
like rotten eggs."

"Charlie! That's rude!" I said,
trying not to laugh.

"I know, but goblins *are* rude, they
fart all the time," he said with a grin.
"Anyway, I'm hoping to get a part in
another film. It's going to be called *The*

Vanishing Carousel."

"That's strange," I said. "A carousel was floating next to our train just now, but it's drifted out of sight. Sophie was on one of the horses. Do you think you could find it and bring Sophie back to the train?"

"Of course I can," said Charlie.

"I hope you are right," said Charlotte. "I want Sophie back. I don't like her being somewhere out there in the night sky. It's not right, and it's all Katherine's fault."

I was about to protest, but I knew Charlotte would not listen to me, and I was beginning to think Charlie might be useful after all. Maybe not all the boys in Mr Pepper's class were as bad as I thought!

Suddenly, I saw an enormous eye

peeping in through our window.

"Dylan, I'm so glad you're here," called Charlie, rushing to the window. "We've got a job to do."

The eye was in the head of a dragon that was flying beside the train! Charlie had already climbed out of the window and was sitting on its back.

"This is Dylan," shouted Charlie. "He pulls the roller coaster at the Pleasure Park. Sometimes Dylan and I fly together at night. He knocks on my bedroom window when he wants to play."

Elroy decided to join in the conversation, but both he and Dylan were talking in a strange language and I couldn't understand what they were saying.

"Elroy! Dylan! Stop talking

Moongook. We've got company tonight – don't be so rude," snapped Marigold.

"Moongook? Sounds more like gobbledygook to me," I said.

"It may sound like gobbledygook

to you, but to magical creatures, it's their normal language," said Marigold. "I can speak Moongook; all fairy godmothers have to learn it."

"Elroy and Dylan sound worried. Please tell me what they were saying," I begged.

"Dylan can smell storm clouds," Marigold explained. "He says they are getting nearer. That means we must find Sophie and the carousel before the storm arrives. Horses are scared of thunder, and they might panic and run away with Sophie."

Charlotte was suddenly at my shoulder. She stamped her feet and said, "Do something, Katherine! I can't believe you've got us into this mess."

I was starting to think Charlotte was right, but I just couldn't think what to do.

"Earlobe, Katherine, remember the earlobe," said Marigold.

"Oh, yes, I'd forgotten about that," I gulped and pulled my earlobe as hard as I could but without much hope of an answer.

"*Snickerdoodles!* What shall I do now?"

Much to my surprise, I knew the answer right away. I had to go with Charlie to find Sophie. My thoughts became action as soon as they entered my head, and I found myself sitting behind Charlie on Dylan's back.

Flying through the Clouds

"Hold on tight! We're off to find Sophie," shouted Dylan.

Dylan's strong wings beat the air and we shot forward like a rocket. Everything became a blur as we dived in and out of the clouds.

"Dragons should have seat belts," I gasped, holding on to Charlie as tightly as I could.

"Don't worry, I've never fallen off,"

said Charlie. "Dragons have a special magnetic force that holds you on. Dylan told me all about it." Charlie leant forward. "Dylan, loop the loop! Let's show Katherine what I mean!"

My heart was in my mouth as Dylan flew straight up then rolled over. For a second, I was hanging upside down at the top of the loop, but I seemed to be glued to Dylan's back. Dylan swooped down at breakneck speed and straightened out, then continued flying as if nothing had happened.

It had been the most terrifying few seconds of my life, but I was filled with a sense of excitement I'd never know before. As shivers ran down my spine, I found myself thinking, *Wow! That was fantastic!*

"The carousel is behind the next cloud," whispered Dylan. "I'll have to get rid of that mischievous moonbeam before it can cause any more trouble."

"How?" I mumbled, still trying to catch my breath.

"You'll see!" laughed Dylan as we flew through the cloud and emerged right in front of Sophie.

With an enormous *whoosh*, smoke shot out of Dylan's nostrils and engulfed Sophie. When the smoke cleared, Sophie was still sitting on the horse, but the moonbeam had gone.

"Mischievous moonbeams cry when smoke gets in their eyes," said Dylan with a satisfied wiggle. "They dissolve into moon rain and fall gently to the ground, their mischief-making days over."

Sophie was unusually silent for a moment and then a torrent of words flew out of her mouth. "How did I get on this carousel? What are you doing on that dragon? Why is Charlie Broccoli here?"

"No time to explain," I said, squeezing my earlobe and shouting,

"*Snickerdoodles!* Sophie, come here!"

And she did. She flew off the horse and landed between Charlie and me, pushing me backwards in the process. It was a tight squeeze and Sophie's nose ended up buried in Charlie's hair.

"Gerroff," growled Charlie, scratching the back of his head.

A very confused Sophie sat bolt upright and snorted. "I can't believe I just sniffed Charlie's hair!" she said, rubbing her nose in disgust.

Dylan said a few words in Moongook to the carousel, and the carousel acknowledged him by playing a tune on the organ.

"Meet Carrie," said Dylan. "She's a very loving carousel. She knows her horses don't like storms and she's glad we warned her. Carrie's going to fly to Oak Tree Hollow and wait for us there. She always goes to the full-moon carnivals.

We watched as Carrie floated away, spinning slowly as she went, and then Dylan set off back towards the train.

In no time at all he was floating next to the carriage window. Dylan curled one of his claws round the window frame, and we climbed safely back on board.

Wizards, Witches & Fairies

As soon as we were in the carriage, Charlotte rushed over to Sophie, her arms open wide.

"What happened to you? Where did you go?" asked Charlotte, giving Sophie a big hug.

The two of them sank down in the corner of the carriage, whispering to each other. Every now and then they looked in my direction, immediately turning away if they saw me looking at them. The word *witch* kept cropping up in their conversation. Finally, they jumped up and glared at me.

"We want to go home," Charlotte cried. "Sophie and I don't want to be on this spooky train with a witch, and we don't want to be friends with you anymore!"

Luckily, just at that moment, Marigold appeared in the carriage. "I promised you all a magical adventure, and that's exactly what's going to happen. This train's not going home yet," she said. "Stop being mean to Katherine or I'll teach her how to turn you both into frogs."

I'd been hurt by the comments my friends had made, and for a split second the thought of turning them into frogs seemed quite appealing. Then I saw the look of horror in their eyes, and that thought quickly disappeared.

"Don't worry, I'd never do it, even if I could," I said. "You're my friends and I love you. I haven't changed. I'm still the same person you've always known."

"Well, if Katherine won't change you into frogs, I will," growled an angry

Charlie Broccoli. "You're both being very spiteful." And with that, a wand appeared in Charlie's hand and he pointed it at my friends.

"Hold on," I yelped, jumping in front of Charlie. "Charlotte and Sophie are scared. They're just saying these things because they don't understand what's happening. Come to think of it, neither do I, and since when could you do magic, Charlie Broccoli?"

"I can see the time has come for an explanation. Sit down everyone and be quiet," commanded Marigold.

Sophie and Charlotte crossed their arms and sat down with a loud *humph* and glared at Marigold. Charlie and I just stood there in silence.

"I know you've always thought your grandma does strange things,"

Marigold began. "You even asked her if she was a witch. Well, now I can tell you, she is a witch!"

"I knew it, I knew I was right!" I hooted.

"Yes, you're right; your grandma found it very difficult keeping that secret from you. She'd wanted to tell you she was a witch for a long time. But I've got more to tell you: witches run in families, so it's not surprising that your mum is a witch too."

"Noooo!" I gasped. "That's not possible, she's so normal."

"And your dad's a wizard," continued Marigold, ignoring my comment. "So, what do you think you are?"

"A witch, I guess," I said with a gulp and flopped down on the bench.

"I've known I was a wizard since my eighth birthday; that's why I can do magic," said Charlie. "My mum and dad are a witch and wizard too. Being a wizard is pretty cool."

"I'm sure it is, but this is the first time I've heard that I'm a witch, and I'm eight and a half. Why didn't anyone tell me before?

"Your mum and dad love living at the Buttercup Bakery, and they wanted you to enjoy a normal life while you were young," said Marigold. "Now you know you're a witch, nothing will ever be quite the same."

"I don't feel like a witch – not that I know how a witch should feel. Are you sure you're not teasing me?"

"I'm not teasing you," said Marigold. "You'll soon get used to it.

Your parents knew I was taking you on a magical adventure tonight, and we agreed this would be a good time to tell you the truth."

"I suppose it is," I agreed, "but it's been like jumping in the deep end of the swimming pool when you can't even swim. Anyway, why are you a fairy and not a witch? It seems odd that you and Grandma Daisy are best friends, when she's a witch and you're a fairy?"

Many questions were tumbling into my mind.

"It's not odd at all," declared Marigold. "Witches and fairies are often best friends."

Village in the Trees

I could see Charlotte and Sophie were still struggling to understand what was happening. I was too, but I hoped we'd all learn to accept the situation in the end.

Elroy broke the tension by trumpeting loudly. "Oak Tree Hollow ahead. Stand by for landing."

He rolled gently to a halt, and Dylan landed next to us. Carrie had already arrived and was waiting for us, lights flashing and organ playing.

We'd arrived on a grassy meadow next to a wood of majestic oak trees. Each tree had a platform resting on its strong branches, and on those platforms were colourful tree houses.

Walkways spread through the trees, and a whole fairyland village was suspended above the ground. Strings of lights twinkled in the leaves, and a barn owl was sitting on the roof of a house. It was a totally magical sight.

Windows lit up, doors opened, and out of each tree house emerged a woodland fairy. The fairies stepped off the platforms into thin air and gracefully floated down to the ground.

Soon our train was surrounded by excited fairies singing *Happy Birthday* to Sophie.

Sophie beamed with delight and waved to the fairies. In all the excitement, she seemed to have stopped worrying that I was a witch, and that made me very happy.

I looked across at Charlie Broccoli. He'd been very quiet since he told us he was a wizard. Like the rest of us, he'd been watching everything that was happening, but I thought he looked a little sad. It's not every day you have to reveal your secret. I knew exactly how that felt.

"I'm going to find space to stretch out my tail," Dylan announced. "The fairies will expect a thrilling ride tonight." He flew to the other side of the meadow. In no time at all, an enormous roller coaster appeared. Dylan was looking very pleased with himself, proudly sitting at the front of a string of coaches. He was waiting for the evening's fun to begin.

"I'm sure Wheelie will be rolling in any time now," said Elroy. "He never misses a full-moon carnival."

As he spoke, we saw a big wheel spinning out of the sky. It landed near Dylan and placed its four enormous legs firmly on the ground.

Wheelie began to revolve and for a few seconds was just a blur of light, but when the spinning stopped, we could see each spoke, and the gondola was covered in multicoloured lights.

I was spellbound. I didn't know where to look next. The carnival was sprinkling itself on the ground like confetti. Tumbling out of the sky were hot-dog stands, ice-cream vans and candyfloss carts, not to mention a variety of side stalls and games. Soon the air was full of music and mouth-watering smells. As the last stall landed, the fairies rushed forward to enjoy the fun.

"Your birthday surprise is ready for you to explore," said Marigold, bringing us back to reality. "I'll come and find you later. You don't want to get tangled up in the tents and rides when the magic ends and they fly back home, do you?"

"No, we don't! We'll look out for you," I said.

We all leapt out of the carriage and rushed into the meadow. Sophie and Charlotte seemed as eager as I was to explore the carnival, I hoped that meant we were still best friends.

Chapter Eleven

Santa's Sleigh

As we entered the carnival, cheering woodland fairies surrounded Sophie. Sophie reached out to grab Charlotte's hand as she tried to wriggle her way out of the crush, but then she and Charlotte were both swept away by the crowd.

Moments later, they found themselves on a stage, sitting on thrones. Charlie and I were watching all this activity from a distance.

"I think the fairies are going to crown Sophie Carnival Queen," I gasped.

And, sure enough, a trumpet sounded and a fairy placed a crown on Sophie's head. The cheering grew louder and I could see Sophie loved being the centre of attention.

After making sure the crown was firmly on her head, Sophie stood up and

waved to the crowd. Being crowned the Carnival Queen was the best birthday present Sophie could have wished for.

Santa's sleigh, pulled by Rudolph, floated in front of the stage. Sophie and Charlotte were directed to climb on board. I couldn't hear what they were saying, but it looked like they were enjoying every minute.

"The sleigh is on loan from Santa, he's let us borrow it for ten minutes," announced a fairy. "Rudolph is going to take our Carnival Queen on a tour of the carnival."

With Sophie and Charlotte safely seated in the sleigh, the fairy shouted, "Sophie, remember to wave!"

"I will," Sophie replied joyfully, and off went the sleigh, with Sophie and Charlotte smiling happily and waving to everyone. Charlie and I were left standing by ourselves.

"They'll be gone for ten minutes," I said, "so I'm going for a ride on the big wheel. I'll be able to see the whole carnival when I get to the top. Do you want to come with me, Charlie?"

"S'pose so," mumbled Charlie. He didn't sound keen, but I was glad he'd said yes, because I had lots of questions to ask him.

We climbed into our gondola and locked the safety bar in place.

"Hold on tight," said Wheelie as he began to turn.

"Charlie, what was the first thing you did when your parents told you that you were a wizard?" I gabbled. I was longing to hear his answer.

Watermelons and Goblins

Charlie laughed as he remembered the moment. "I made a mess in Dad's shop," he answered. "You have no idea what a box of watermelons can do!"

Charlie's laugh was infectious and I started to giggle.

"Mum and Dad gave me a wand, and I waved it around yelling *boom – bash – bosh*. No idea why I chose those words, I was just excited, I guess.

Unfortunately, I pointed the wand at the watermelons and they exploded! There was pink gloop all over the walls."

Charlie's mum and dad own the greengrocer's shop in Puddington. We always buy our fruit and vegetables there, but I never guessed they were a family of wizards.

"What did your parents do about it?" I asked. I had an image of the shop in my head – it was a very yucky sight.

"Well, apart from doubling up with laughter, Dad waved his wand and said *'Mundare muros'* and the walls were clean in a flash. That was the first spell I ever saw my dad do, and I learnt it fast. It's very useful. Every time I make a mess, I can clean it up in a second. You'll be learning spells now, Katherine – they're great fun."

"Will I get a wand?" I asked.

"Dunno," said Charlie. "Maybe? You'll just have to wait and see what happens."

"That's not very helpful, Charlie," I moaned.

While we'd been chatting, the wheel had been slowly turning and we were right at the top. I was looking down at the fairground and I caught sight of Sophie and Charlotte. Santa's sleigh had stopped by the carousel to let Sophie and Charlotte jump out. They were giggling happily.

I saw Charlie suddenly hold his nose. "Yuck! Can you smell rotten eggs? I hope it's not what I think it is – but if it is, we're in for trouble."

I sniffed as hard as I could and got a whiff of something nasty. Then we heard a loud *thrrrrp pfffft* and the most appalling smell I'd ever smelt filled the air!

"Goblins!" shrieked Charlie as he swung round to look at the gondola behind us.

"I knew it! It's the fire-breathing goblins from my film – the two spiteful ones that set my hair on fire. They're up to mischief, I'm sure. They're looking for something to steal – probably a horse. Goblins always steal horses when they can."

I turned round and saw two ugly faces staring at me. Little flicks of fire popped out of their mouths as they curled their lips menacingly.

The big wheel continued to turn and we were getting near the ground.

Icy Magic

"Don't worry," Charlie whispered in my ear. "Last time I met those goblins I didn't know I was a wizard, but I can handle this situation now. As soon as we are on the ground, I'll send them back to the dark cave they live in."

The goblins must have known what Charlie was thinking. They stood up in their gondola and jumped over our heads before the big wheel had stopped turning. They were cackling like geese, spitting flames and farting as they ran off into the crowd. We quickly lost sight of them, much to our concern!

"Oh peanuts! That's the last thing we need," groaned Charlie. "A pair of fire-breathing goblins on the loose. We'd better find Sophie and Charlotte as soon as possible. Those goblins are going to cause trouble."

"I saw the girls at the carousel. Let's go there," I said, setting off immediately.

The carousel was already in motion when we arrived. We waited to see if Sophie and Charlotte were on board and, sure enough, they came into sight, sitting on two horses next to each other.

We waved like mad to catch

their attention. The girls waved back and disappeared again as the carousel continued turning. Next time round they waved again, but to our horror, on the horses behind them we saw the two goblins.

"Carrie Carousel, can you hear me?" I whispered. "There are two goblins riding on your horses."

"Yes, I know. I'm keeping an eye on them," Carrie replied.

I could hardly believe it. I could hear Carrie's reply in my head. Suddenly a whole new world was opening before me. Maybe being a witch was not so bad after all.

"Charlie," I said. "We've got to do something quickly. The girls have no idea there are two goblins behind them."

"Keep calm. I've got a plan," said

Charlie. "I'm going to turn the goblins to ice and leave them stuck to the horses. When the carnival ends, Carrie will fly away home and drop the goblins somewhere in the clouds. They'll have to find their own way to their cave from wherever they land."

"Sounds like a good idea," I said, "but won't they get hurt when they hit the ground?"

"They might end up with bits of ice in their bum," laughed Charlie, "but goblins are very rubbery; when they hit the ground they'll just bounce!"

"Time to cast your spell, Charlie. The goblins look as if they're about to leap on Sophie and Charlotte!"

Both Charlie and I heard Carrie's words in our head and Charlie took out his wand and yelled, *"Coboli frigidus!"*

The nearest goblin turned to ice immediately, but the second goblin only turned to ice from the waist down. His arms were still waving and he was spitting fire.

I squeezed my earlobe and yelled, *"Snickerdoodles, Coboli frigidus!"* It was lucky Charlie's spell was very short and easy to remember.

As soon as I said those words, the last flicker of flame disappeared from the goblin's mouth, and he was frozen solid with his arms still raised above his head.

"I'm very impressed!" said Charlie. "You've got the hang of being a witch already. You're like me – a quick learner. You'll be going to summer school this year. It's two weeks of trying out all kinds of spells. It can get a bit messy, but it's great fun. I had a wonderful time last year; I made loads of new friends and I even had my first ride on a broomstick."

"Broomstick?" That word sent my

head spinning. I'd never thought about a broomstick until Charlie mentioned it, and now it was ringing in my brain like a bell! Broomsticks! Wands! Being a witch was getting more exciting every minute.

I was longing to hear more about the summer school, but the carousel was slowing down, and I had to get my breath back before it stopped. Sophie and Charlotte were right in front of us when Carrie came to a halt and the girls clambered down and ran to greet us.

They had no idea there had been two evil goblins on the horses behind them. Charlie winked at me and we decided to keep that information to ourselves. We thought Sophie and Charlotte had suffered enough shocks for one day. We didn't want to upset them again.

"Sophie, I think you should choose what we do next. You are the birthday girl," I said.

"Oooo, yes please! Let's all go on the roller coaster," said Sophie. "I'm sure Dylan will give us a scary ride. After that we can have hot dogs before Marigold comes to find us."

And that's exactly what we did.

Myrtle and Mimosa

After our tummy-tingling ride on the roller coaster, we took a few minutes to get our breath back, then we set off to find the hot-dog stall.

I asked for mayo with mine. Sophie decided on barbecue sauce and Charlotte went for tomato ketchup.

What are you going to have on yours, Charlie?" I asked.

"That's easy," he replied, "a

splodge of everything, please!"

As we stood there devouring
our hot dogs, I looked at Sophie and
Charlotte. I wondered what they were
thinking, but before I could ask them,
Sophie began to speak.

"Katherine – Charlotte and I want to say we think it's cool that you are a witch. We've talked about it and we know you haven't really changed. We're sorry we were nasty to you earlier, but it was rather a shock."

I felt tears running down my face, but they were tears of happiness. "I'm so glad you said that," I gulped. "I couldn't bear it if we fell out. We've always been friends, and I want to go on being best friends, for ever."

"So do we," said Charlotte, "and we'd like Charlie to be our friend too. He helped you rescue Sophie and that makes him pretty okay with us, even though he's in Mr Pepper's class."

At that moment, Marigold appeared. "Nearly time to go home," she said, "but I've got one last birthday surprise for you. Follow me everyone."

We dutifully trotted after Marigold until we came to the fairy grotto, although Charlie had been lagging behind us.

As we were about to enter the

grotto, Charlie piped up: "I'm off! Marigold said it's okay for Dylan to take me home. I love flying with him through the night sky."

"*Marigold said it's okay.* Well, lucky you," I said mockingly. "What do I care if you go? We can manage without you, Charlie Broccoli."

"Meow!" said Sophie. "Someone's not happy!"

I could feel myself going bright red, but I had to admit I was sorry Charlie was leaving. I'd got used to him being around.

Seeing my disappointment, Marigold explained that she was Charlie's fairy godmother as well as mine. She had promised him that he could fly home with Dylan instead of travelling on the train with three girls.

"What's wrong with being with three girls? We don't bite!" I snapped, but I regretted that comment as soon as I'd made it and quickly added, "but I suppose we have our fairy godmother in common. I'll see you in school next week, then!"

"See ya!" called Charlie, and with that, he dashed away to join Dylan.

When we entered the grotto, we found ourselves in an enormous cave with sparkling white stalactites hanging from the roof. A turquoise

pool shimmered in front of us, and standing by the pool were two woodland fairies.

"Meet Myrtle and Mimosa, my two lovely nieces," said Marigold. "They've just graduated from college and are now fully trained fairy godmothers. They need two young people to look after, and I thought Sophie and Charlotte would be perfect for that."

"You mean I'm going to have my own fairy godmother, just like Katherine?" gasped Sophie. "My very own fairy godmother?" she squeaked.

"Yes, Sophie, your very own fairy godmother," said Marigold with a happy smile.

"And me too?" asked a bewildered Charlotte. "But it's not my birthday."

"I know," said Marigold, "but both you and Sophie passed the test of accepting Katherine as a witch, so you both deserve a fairy godmother. Not every child would have done that."

"Oh, wow!" gasped Charlotte, who could hardly believe her luck.

"Although they've graduated from college, Myrtle and Mimosa still have a lot to learn, so, for the first year I will be their mentor. Don't expect them to do everything I can do," chuckled Marigold.

Myrtle and Mimosa floated over to the girls and gave them a kiss. "That kiss is our promise to look after you," they explained.

I have never seen Sophie and Charlotte look so blissfully happy.

Chapter Fifteen

Candyfloss and Kisses

We were on the way back to the train when we saw the candyfloss cart. It was too tempting to resist, but Marigold decided to go on ahead with Myrtle and Mimosa. We waited impatiently for our large clouds of sugary pink fluffiness to be spun on a stick before racing after them.

By the time we arrived at the train, Myrtle and Mimosa were talking to

Elroy. I'm sure he was blushing, because his cheeks were the same colour as our candyfloss.

"Myrtle and Mimosa are practising Moongook," explained Marigold. "Flying with magical creatures is part of their job now. Elroy gets embarrassed when he meets new fairy godmothers for the first time."

"I can see why," I laughed, as I watch Myrtle and Mimosa kiss and cuddle him. Elroy's ears began flapping so wildly, I thought he was about to fly away.

We climbed into our carriage and looked out of the window. The woodland fairies were flying back to their tree houses. They landed on the walkways, and stood there, waiting to wave goodbye to us.

Dylan was the first carnival ride to take off. He shot into the air, looped the loop and disappeared into the distance. I'm sure I saw Charlie waving to us.

Wheelie and Carrie were the next to leave, and then all the stalls sailed into the air like umbrellas blown by the wind. The meadow became a waving field of grass and summer flowers again, not a trace of the carnival remained.

"Goodbye Sophie," called Myrtle. "Call my name if you need me."

"Goodbye Charlotte," said Mimosa, "Remember, I'll come when you call."

We were soon in the air, waving goodbye to the woodland fairies. After the most surprising and thrilling night of our lives, we were finally on our way home.

I began this adventure as Katherine Baker, an ordinary kid who loved baking, and I was returning as Katherine Baker, a witch. It was going to take me a long time to get used to that!

The journey home only lasted long enough for Sophie and Charlotte to give me a big hug.

"You're not like the wicked witches we've seen in films, you're just like Samantha, the one with the twitchy nose. She was lovely, even though she was only make-believe," they said.

"I love Samantha," I said with a happy sigh.

Before we knew it, we were outside my den and back in our night clothes. The snow had gone and Marigold was saying goodbye to Elroy.

We all joined in and Elroy got so

many kisses and hugs from three very happy girls, that his cheeks began to turn bright pink again.

"I've got to get back to Puddington Pleasure Park," said Elroy. "I'm sure I'll see you there one day." And with that, Elroy flapped his ears and took off.

As we watched Elroy disappear into the distance, Marigold handed me a long thin box.

"You've passed your first test with flying colours. You no longer need to say *snickerdoodles* to cast a spell," she said. "You will find everything you need in this box."

wands and Butterflies

I was trembling with excitement as I opened the box. "Marigold, it's wonderful!" I gasped, as I took out a wand and held it in the air. "Now I feel like a witch."

"The oldest tree in Oak Tree Hollow donated a piece of wood to make that wand," Marigold explained. "It's a very wise wand, perfect for a young witch who has a lot to learn."

"Thank you, Marigold, it's fantastic, but I only know one spell, and that was the spell I heard Charlie use," I said.

"Don't worry, the wand knows all the basic spells and you will learn more as the weeks go by."

I gave Marigold a big hug, and then my phone started to ring. I'd left it in my den when we rushed out to play in the snow.

"Go and answer it," said Marigold. "I've got things to do. I'll see you again very soon."

I dashed into my den and picked up my phone.

"Hello sweetie," I heard Mum say. "Dad and I just want to let you know how proud we are. You coped with all the challenges thrown at you tonight.

We have so much to talk about in the morning. Enjoy your sleepover, you've earned it. Sweet dreams."

I'd no sooner said goodnight to Mum when the phone rang again. This time it was Grandma.

"Marigold has just popped in to tell me you did very well tonight. I'm so happy I don't have to keep secrets from you anymore."

"So am I, Grandma. Deep down, I always knew you were a witch! I'll come to see you tomorrow."

Sophie was already tucking in to one of the cupcakes I'd made for her birthday. I'd put a sugar-paste butterfly on each one.

I'd seen Marigold cast a spell on sugar-paste butterflies. She brought them to life and made them fly.

Maybe my wand knows that spell,
I thought. *It will be a wonderful way to
use it for the first time.*

When I pointed my wand at the
butterflies, Sophie cried out, "Watch
where you're pointing that thing. I don't
trust you with a wand – you can't even
hit a tennis ball properly."

"I'll be careful," I promised. "I don't want anything to go wrong tonight. I'm only going to make the butterflies fly off the cupcakes. That can't do any harm, can it?"

To my delight, the sugar-paste butterflies flew into the air. They fluttered round my den. They were lovely for about twenty seconds. Then, they quickly became annoying. One even landed on Sophie's nose!

I couldn't bear the thought of turning them back to sugar paste, so I opened the door and told them to fly into the orchard and sit on a branch until the sun came up! They obeyed immediately.

I was thrilled beyond words.

"My wand works," I squealed in delight. "Now I believe I am a witch.

We've had such an exciting evening, all I want to do is go to sleep now – I'm exhausted!"

We snuggled into our sleeping bags and started to talk, but that didn't last for long.

The next thing I heard was Dad's voice saying, "Good morning sleepy-heads, I think it's time you woke up; it's half-past ten. Breakfast is waiting for you in the kitchen. Who wants pancakes with maple syrup?" And then Dad was gone, leaving the door wide open with the sun streaming in.

I sat up slowly and rubbed my eyes. Sophie and Charlotte started to wriggle and snuffle as the bright morning light woke them up.

"Did all that really happen last

night?" mumbled Sophie. "I know I said I wanted to do something different on my birthday, but last night was *really* different."

"It certainly was," agreed Charlotte, giving a big, sleepy yawn. "We went flying in a land train, then you were kidnapped by a mischievous moonbeam, and Charlie Broccoli flew to your rescue on a dragon. Not only that, but you were then crowned Carnival Queen!"

"I know, totally unreal, wasn't it!" said Sophie. "But the best bit was when Marigold introduced us to our fairy godmothers. Can you believe that? We have our very own fairy godmother."

"I'm pleased about that, but you seem to have forgotten I'm a witch." I waved my wand and yelled, "Pillow

107

fight!"

Immediately, we were holding pillows in our hands and they seemed to have a mind of their own. They hurled themselves around, furiously trying to hit the other two pillows.

We were dragged out of our sleeping bags and ended up, rolling on the floor in a tangled heap, giggling wildly.

"Last night was the most amazing night of my life," I said, as we sat on the floor, out of breath. "I can't wait to find out what's going to happen next. We're going to have such fun together. Tomorrow won't just be different; it will be **magic!**"

Picture book by the same author

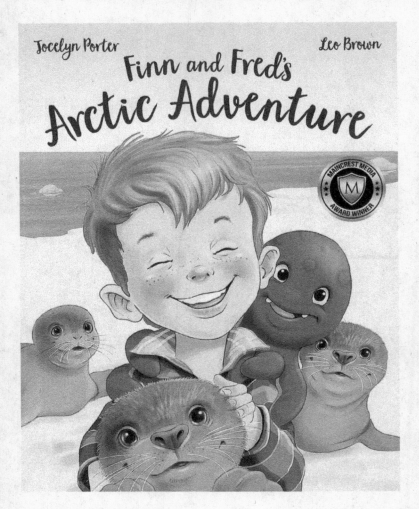

"My bus takes off with a sonic boom, straight through the wall and out of my room..."

Finn and Fred Octopus are off on a magical adventure to the Arctic. They meet a kindly seal, a hungry polar bear and an angry walrus. The whales sing to Finn, and Finn arrives home with an important message to share...

"Packed with adventure and excitement that children will love, *Finn and Fred* has a powerful environmental message that couldn't be more needed. I thought *Finn and Fred* was excellent." ★ ★ ★ ★ ★ Linda Hill, lindasbookbag.com

100% of the sale price of this book bought at the Cornish Seal Sanctuary will go directly to the Sanctuary.
10% of the profit of this book bought elsewhere will also go to the Cornish Seal Sanctuary.

FullMediaLtd

SEA LIFE TRUST — Cornish Seal Sanctuary

£6.99

9 781916 896840

The King Who Didn't Like Snow

Written by Jocelyn Porter   Illustrated by Michael S Kane

Wizard Bert waved his wand and everything in Cornovia went topsy-turvy!

King Mark is a higgledy-piggledy king who gets into a pickle every day. "Do something, Bert!" he shouts, and Wizard Bert, with his sidekick, Broderick the bookworm, always saves the day. When snow falls on Windy Hill Castle, everyone is delighted - except for King Mark! King Mark doesn't like snow and starts to sulk. Will Bert and Broderick save the day again? Will King Mark walk into trouble? Do the children of Windy Hill Village have the answer...?

"Brilliant, educational, and fun! Loved it!"
readersfavorite.com ★★★★★

"An engaging story which will encourage children to talk about their fears." thebookbag.co.uk ★★★★

FullMediaLtd

£6.99

9 781916 896826

Three Times Round the Corkscrew Tree

A Katherine Baker Adventure

By Jocelyn Porter

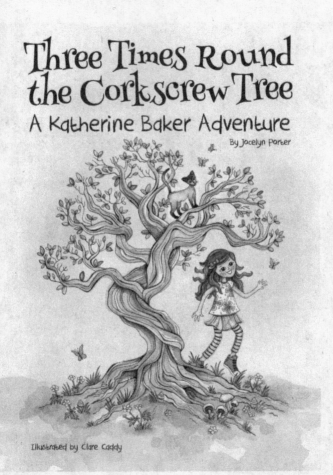

Illustrated by Clare Caddy

Katherine closed her eyes and imagined a magical world

Katherine is a girl with a big imagination. When she isn't baking she likes playing with her friends in her den. Treasure hunting in the orchard is their favourite game! One day they found something exciting in the roots of the crazy corkscrew tree. Grandma Daisy believes in fairies and says strange things happen at the Buttercup Bakery because it's so old. Katherine definitely doesn't believe in fairies and ignores her grandma's stories. However, when Grandma's spooky friend arrives strange things start to happen to Katherine...

£4.99 ISBN: 978-1-909714-57-1

FSC 9 781909 714571

Services for writers

As well as publishing high-quality children's picture books and chapter books, Full Media Ltd offer a range of professional services for writers.

We can assist with:

Proofreading
Editing
Layout and formatting
Web design
Publishing

For more information visit full-media.co.uk

Goodbye - Happy Reading!

Goodbye & Happy Reading!